CUDDLE&READ

This book belongs to

_____

*To those who have shared their love with me through the years,
especially my children: Ilyse, Ilijah, and Ian. I love you back!*
—T.J.M.

For Mama, Papa, and "Little Bits" Ford
—A.B.

STERLING and the distinctive Sterling logo are registered trademarks of Sterling Publishing Co., Inc.

Library of Congress Cataloging-in-Publication Data Available

Lot #:
2 4 6 8 10 9 7 5 3 1
09/10

Published by Sterling Publishing Co., Inc.

387 Park Avenue South, New York, NY 10016
Text © 2011 by Tara Jaye Morrow
Illustrations © 2011 by Aaron Boyd

Designed and produced for Sterling by COLOR-BRIDGE BOOKS, LLC, Brooklyn, NY

Distributed in Canada by Sterling Publishing
c/o Canadian Manda Group, 165 Dufferin Street
Toronto, Ontario, Canada M6K 3H6
Distributed in the United Kingdom by GMC Distribution Services
Castle Place, 166 High Street, Lewes, East Sussex, England BN7 1XU
Distributed in Australia by Capricorn Link (Australia) Pty. Ltd.
P.O. Box 704, Windsor, NSW 2756, Australia

Printed in China

Sterling ISBN 978-1-4027-4315-3

For information about custom editions, special sales, premium and
corporate purchases, please contact Sterling Special Sales
Department at 800-805-5489 or specialsales@sterlingpublishing.com.

Panda's Valentine's Day

By Tara Jaye Morrow • Illustrated by Aaron Boyd

STERLING

New York / London
www.sterlingpublishing.com/kids

It was Valentine's Day, and that meant one very important thing. It was time for Panda and Mama to make valentine cards for each other. Panda thought long and hard about what kind of valentine to make.

He wanted it to be pretty, just like Mama.
He wanted it to be fun, just like Mama.
And he wanted it to have a lot of love inside.
Just like Mama.

Panda sat down at his desk. He took out sheets of pink and red paper, some crayons, scissors, glue, and a piece of red ribbon he had saved from school.

Panda had also been collecting beads in a jar and he wanted
to put some on Mama's valentine.

First Panda tried to cut out a heart from the red paper.
One side was bigger than the other, but Panda thought
maybe Mama wouldn't notice.

Then Panda tried to glue the ribbon around the card. But it was so thin it kept tearing. Panda tried to glue the beads to the edges of his valentine, but that didn't look very nice.

Panda decided he would write the words for the inside of Mama's valentine on a slip of paper. But when he tried to glue it inside, it wouldn't stick.

Panda's valentine looked nothing like he wanted it to look. It wasn't pretty like his mama. It wasn't fun like his mama.

And he didn't even get to put the love inside the way he had planned.

Panda threw his valentine in the wastebasket. He wasn't sure what he was going to give his mama for Valentine's Day.

Panda put on his boots, his coat, a hat, and a scarf and went outside to think. There was a dusting of fresh snow on the ground.

He made some little snowballs and threw them at a tree.
He tried building a snowman but the snow was too wet.
Panda was feeling very discouraged.

Panda sat down in the snow outside the kitchen window and waved his arms up and down. He had made a big heart in the snow.

Mama looked out the window and smiled. Then she called Panda to come inside.

Mama was waiting for Panda in the kitchen.
She had hot chocolate and warm cookies
shaped like hearts with little red sprinkles
on top.

Panda's mama made the very best cookies in
the whole world.

When Panda sat down, he saw the valentine Mama had made for him on the table. Panda picked it up and looked down at the floor. It was really nice.

"That's not the face of my happy valentine, Panda," Mama said.

"I'm sad because I didn't finish your valentine card, Mama. I tried to make it pretty and fun like you, but it just kept falling apart."

"Did you finish any of it, Panda?" asked Mama.
"Only the words," he answered.
"May I see?" she asked.

Panda ran upstairs and got the slip of paper with the words he had written for his mama. Then he brought it to her.

Mama read Panda's words.

My mama is pretty.
My mama is fun.
Of all Panda mamas,
mine's the best one.

Hearts are so pretty.
And candy is sweet.
I love you, Mama,
from your head
to your feet.

Mama gave Panda a big bear hug.
"Sorry I didn't give you the best valentine ever,"
said Panda.

"But you did," said Mama. She took Panda's hand and led him outside.

There in the snow was the heart Panda had made.
"See?" said Mama. "And the words you wrote are my
favorite part."
"They are?" asked Panda, surprised.
"Of course," said Mama. "The words have all your love
in them!"

"Happy Valentine's Day, Mama!" said Panda.
"Happy Valentine's Day, sweet Panda!" said Mama.